Summertime

FROM
Porgy and Bess

by GEORGE GERSHWIN,
DuBOSE *and* DOROTHY HEYWARD,
and IRA GERSHWIN

paintings by MIKE WIMMER

ALADDIN PAPERBACKS
New York London Toronto Sydney Singapore

Special thanks and gratitude to
Gloria and Jerry Pinkney,
who through their work in children's literature
and their examples as parents and teachers
have given us so much.

— M.W.

First Aladdin Paperbacks edition June 2002

Summertime © 1999 based on the Composition "Summertime"

from the folk opera entitled *Porgy and Bess* by George Gershwin,

DuBose and Dorothy Heyward, and Ira Gershwin

© 1935 (renewed 1962) George Gershwin Music,

Ira Gershwin Music and The DuBose and Dorothy Heyward Memorial Fund

Used by permission.

Illustrations copyright © 1999 by Mike Wimmer

ALADDIN PAPERBACKS

An imprint of Simon & Schuster

Children's Publishing Division

1230 Avenue of the Americas

New York, NY 10020

Also available in a Simon and Schuster Books for Young Readers hardcover edition.

Designed by Heather Wood

The text for this book is set in Horley Old Style Semi-Bold Italic.

The paintings were rendered in oil paint on linen canvas;

they were inspired by the work of Winslow Homer.

Printed in Hong Kong

2   4   6   8   10   9   7   5   3   1

The Library of Congress has cataloged the hardcover edition as follows:

Library of Congress Catalog Card Number: 98-88194

ISBN 0-689-80719-8

ISBN 0-689-85047-6 (Aladdin pbk.)

Elijah and Lauren,
I sang this song to you every night;
now I give it to you forever.

—M.W.

Summertime

and the livin' is easy,

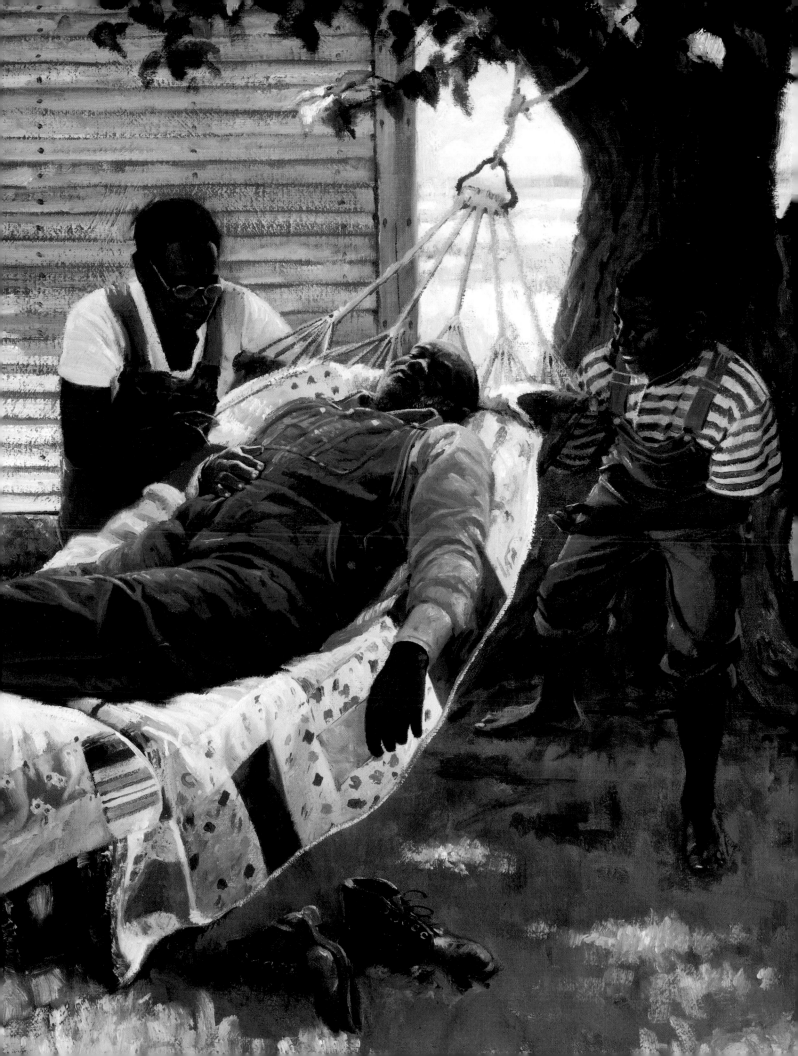

Fish are jumpin',

and the cotton is high.

Oh your daddy's rich,

*and your ma
is good lookin',*

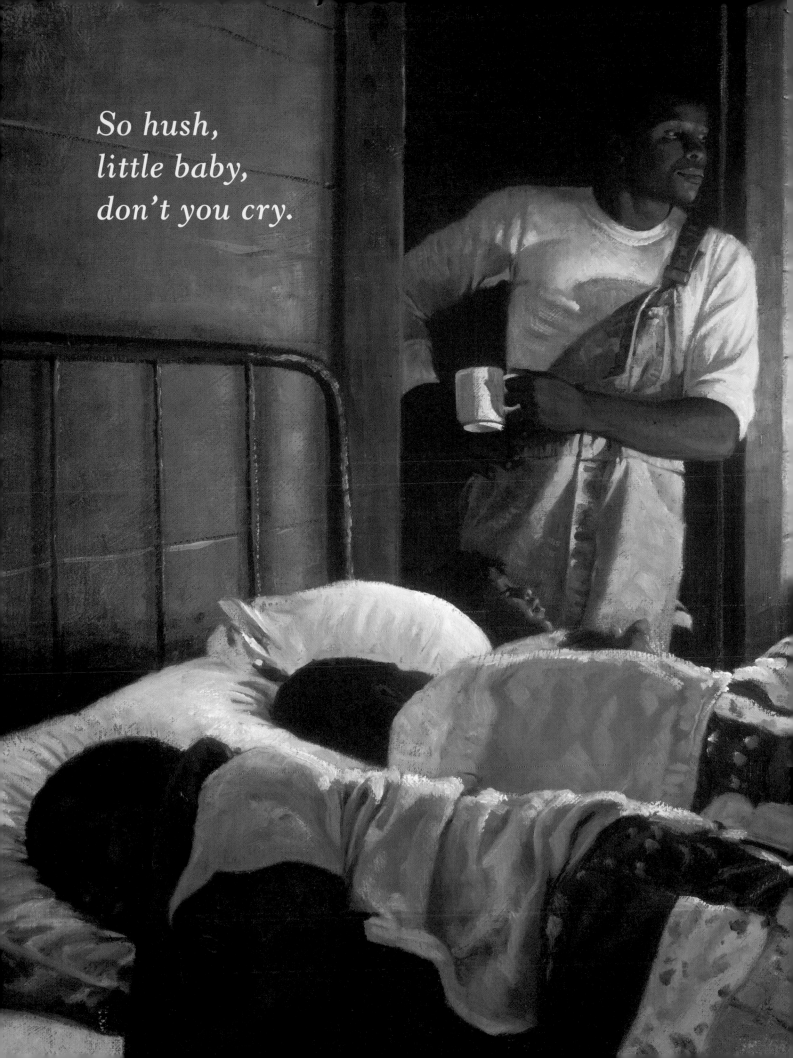

*So hush,
little baby,
don't you cry.*

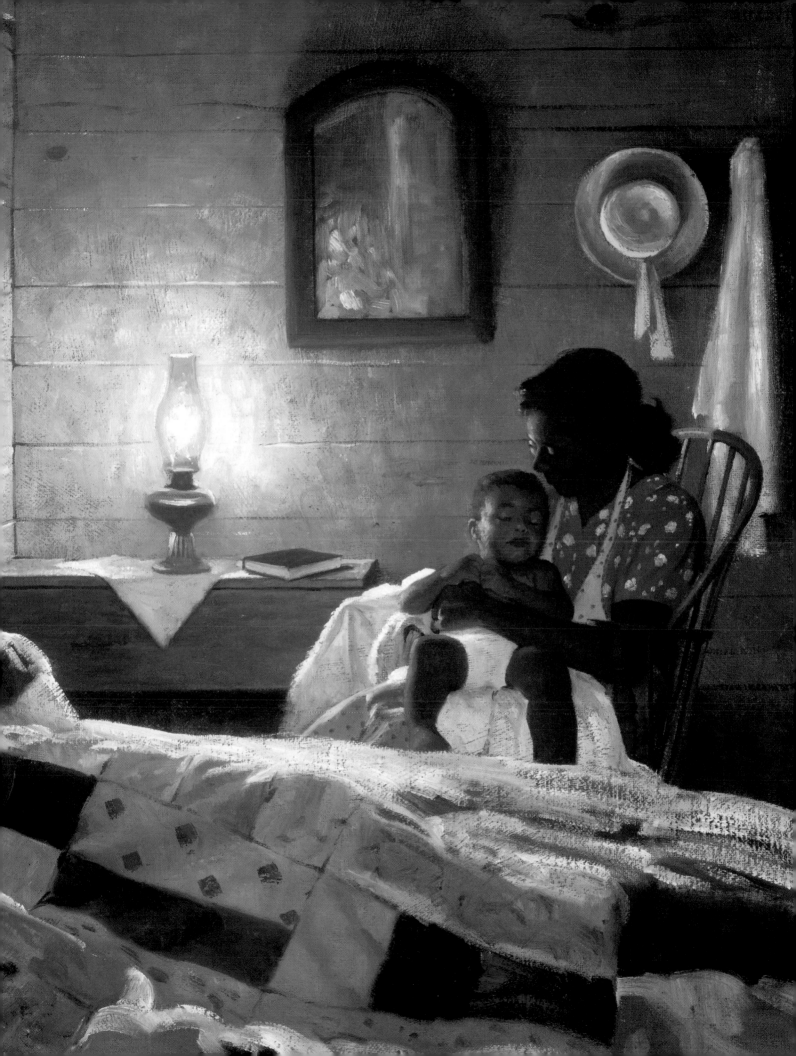

One of these mornin's

*you're goin' to
rise up singin',*

Then you'll spread your wings

and you'll take
to the sky.

But till that mornin'

there's a nothin' can harm you

with Daddy and Mama standin' by.

Summertime
FROM *Porgy and Bess*

by GEORGE GERSHWIN, DuBOSE *and* DOROTHY HEYWARD, *and* IRA GERSHWIN